Poems for the Young and Young at Heart

LINA SAWITZ

Poems for the Young and Young at Heart
Copyright © 2024 by Lina Sawitz

Tellwell Talent
www.tellwell.ca

ISBN
978-1-77941-851-7 (Paperback)

Table of Contents

Dedication

To my beautiful, intelligent, kind and loving granddaughter. I am so happy that you love all creatures, big and small. You are a special gift to me and your parents! Always remember that I love you more today than I did yesterday, but not as much as I will tomorrow!

Grandmother Lina

Acknowledgments

I would like to acknowledge and thank the people that encouraged and supported me throughout this process!

First my family. My daughter Stephanie who encouraged me and had faith in me! My granddaughter Maddy, who gave me lots of hugs and kisses and wanted to write her own stories! My son-in-law who looked after my family in good time and bad.

I would also like to thank my Wescott family. Laurenn MacDonald, Jessica Thompson, and Arsh Kaur for recommending me for this dream of mine to be fulfilled. Dyan Garcia, for typing all my poems! For finding pictures and for so many other things.

I would also like to thank Amanda Lopez and The Chartwell Foundation for helping me publish my book and making my wish come true.

Chartwell Wescott: My Home

We came here to Wescott,
From far and from near
To live here together
Without any fear.
The staff are so caring,
And loving and kind
They keep us all sharing,
Our talents and minds
They share in our laughter,
And sorrows and tears
They feed our food cravings,
And chase away our fears.
So, thank you for keeping us,
Close to your hearts.
And coming to treat us,
With cute little puppies,
And cookies, doughnuts, and tarts

January

The first month of the year,
Will you bring us happy days,
Or days that we shall fear.

Will you bring us sunshine, Will you bring us rains?
Will you bring us jack frost, to paint our windowpanes?

Will you bring us snowflakes,
To make our world so white.
Will you bring us strong winds,
That will howl through the night.

Dear first month of the year
Be kind and fill us with good cheer.
To help us all conquer,
The rest of the year

February

February winds are icy cold.
The snow is piling high,
The ground is frozen,
The trees are bare,
The birds can hardly fly.
But my heart sings
My heart rejoices.
My heart I give away.
For in this cold, cold February
We have Valentine's Day

March

March can be snowy.
March can be blowy.
March can be sunny.
March can be funny.
But march is the month when spring appears,
And most of the snow just disappears!

April

April tries to fool us from the very first day.
It says spring is coming, but it seems so far away.

The dark clouds above us, are heavy with rain.
They hang there suspended, ready to open up the drain.
And then it starts pouring, day in and day out,
It seems like the heavens, opened up a spout!

Please sky stop raining, the children all shout
We can't wait for sunshine, to dry us all out.
Then the sun shines so bright
From behind the grey clouds
And tries to surprise us with a beautiful sight!

The rainbows start forming,
And spanning the skies
How lovely the colours
Shining bright in our eyes!

May

May comes slowly like a bride,
Through the meadows full of pride
Wearing long flowing dresses
A wreath of flowers on her tresses.

She caresses the little buds,
And makes them raise their tiny heads.
Then giving each a sunny smile
She continues to walk another mile.

June

Children love the month of June,
For soon they will be running free.
And shouting this chant with glee,
"No more pencils, no more books,
No more teacher's dirty looks!"
But soon they will be missing their friends,
And waiting for summer to come to an end!

July

The sky is exploding,
With colourful light.
It looks like the stars,
Are starting a fight.

The sound is like thunder,
Shaking the earth.
We love to watch fireworks,
Lightning the sky!
What a great celebration,
On the first of July.
When we all wish our country,
A very Happy Birthday!

August

The sun is hot,
The days are bright.
We can stay outside,
From morning till night.

It is a very great month,
For birthday fun.
And swimming and picnics,
And playing in the sun.

Building castles and forts,
And rivers and lakes.
Making turtles and snakes,
For heaven's sakes.

September

September brings us,
Good new friends
School begins,
And summer ends

October

Autumn leaves come tumbling down.
Red, yellow, orange, and brown
They cover the ground at my feet,
And race before me down the street

November

November days
Are crisp and cool,
And we must wear,
Warm clothes to school

December

December is here.
The best month of the year.
It brings us lots of days,
that fill us with cheer.

There is baking Christmas cookies.
And decorating the tree.
And wrapping Christmas presents,
To hide under the tree.

There is laughter and sharing,
And watching the snow fall.
Drifting softly towards us,
And covering the ground.

We hear church bells ringing,
Urging us to come.

To welcome Lord Jesus,
And wish him a Happy Birthday!

St. Patrick's Day

St. Patrick's Day
St. Patrick's Day
Of leprechauns beware
Put a shamrock in your hat,
And find something green to wear!

Two Little Clouds

Two little clouds
One April day
Went sailing across the sky.
They went so fast,
That they bumped their heads
And both began to cry.

The big round sun
Came out and said,
Oh, never mind my dears,
I'll send them all my sunbeams down,
to dry away your tears!

Finger Play

Here's a little bunny, with ears so funny.
And here's his hole, in the ground.
At the first sound he hears
He perks up his ears,
And jumps in the hope in the ground.

Spring

It's Spring, called the Earth.
Walking from the long winter's nap
Let's go out and hop and swing,
Let's raise our heads and let our voices ring.

Welcome, welcome,
Lovely Spring!

It's spring, called the robins,
Looking for some seeds or
Hoping for a fat little worm

It's Spring, called the flowers,
Raising their delicate heads to the sun

It's Spring, called the trees,
Busting with green buds all around

It's Spring, called baby animals,
Coming out to hop and play

It's spring, called the children,
Racing their bikes down the street

It's Spring, sighed the grownups,
Enjoying the sun on their face

I love Bunnies!

I love bunnies.
The big and the small
But I love the chocolate ones,
The best of all

Mother's Day

May gives us a chance,
To thank all our mothers
In a very special way!

No matter where you are,
In the world on that day
You can call your mother,
And wish her a Happy Mother's Day!
You can send her some flowers,
Or a card that will say
I love you dear mother,
And miss you every single day.

Maypole

Run around the Maypole
On a sunny day in May
Let the lovely ribbons,
Flash in and out all the way
Now see if you can do it the other way.
Make sure you don't get tangled,
And lose your way.

Autumn

Apple mellow,
Pumpkins yellow.
What's the time of year?
Leaves are falling.
Natures calling,
Autumn time is here!

Fall

October's the month
When the littlest breeze
Gives us the shower,
Of autumn leaves

Halloween

Witches ride on Hallowe'en
Ooo ooo ooo
Their coats are black,
And their eyes are green.
Ooo ooo ooo
Every witch has big, black hat,
Ooo ooo ooo
And every witch has a big black cat,
Meow meow meow
SCAT!

Christmas

Christmas is coming,
And I'm full of woe.
I wrote Santa a letter,
A long time ago.

But we moved to a new house,
And I wanted Santa to know.
So, I wrote him again,
But I want him to understand.
I'm not greedy or vain,
I just want that one gift.
A little live puppy,
Will do just fine.

We Will Remember You

We will remember,
In the morning light
When the day is breaking
And the sky is bright.

We will remember,
When we look at the sky
And see the doves and eagles,
Flying up so high

We will remember,
At the break of day
When the rising sun
Brightens our way.

We will remember,
When we see the clouds
Drifting slowly with the breeze
Covering the sun with ease

We will remember,
Your beautiful smile
For the image of you
Is always deep in our hearts.
We will remember!

Remember me

Don't remember me with sadness.
Don't remember me with tears,
Just remember all the laughter
We've shared throughout the years.
Now I am contented.
That my life, it was worthwhile.
Knowing that I passed along the way,
And maybe made somebody smile.
When you are walking down the street,
And you've got me on your mind,
I am walking in your footsteps,
Only half a step behind.
So please don't be unhappy,
Just because I'm out of sight.
Remember that I'm with you,
Each morning, noon and night.

The Forest by Maddy

Forest trees breathe in the wind,
All the animals are going to sleep.
Sleep, sleep in the deep, dark woods
The owls hoot!
The leaves rustle in the woods!
The owls' eyes are watching the animals below,
The bats screech as they fly around the woods.
They are looking for some tasty bugs.
Finally, it's morning!
The animals awake,
The owls and the bats go to sleep,
In the deep dark woods!

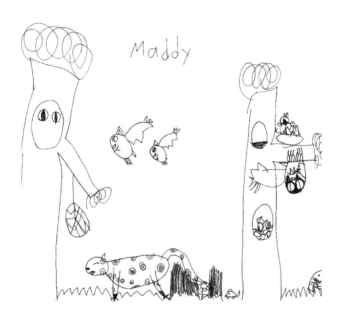

Maddy

I Am a Sea Dragon by Grandma & Maddy

I am a little dragon,
That lives in the sea.
They call me little sea dragon,
Because I have big eyes,
But I cannot see!

On the yellow sand,
I can barely see.
But in the water,
I can see colours from red to purple,
To yellow and green.
Have you ever seen a green fish?
I have and it was very green!
I will see you next time,
Be ready for my next poem.

About the Author

Lina Verbickaite Sawitz was born in Lithuania at the dawn of the Second World War. Her family was moved to Germany as displaced persons, and eventually came to Canada.

They started their lives as immigrants with very little. Lina eventually became a teacher at a time when teachers were in demand. She spent 40 years in a career that she loved. It was through teaching that she found a love of poetry—which she passed on to her daughter and granddaughter. It has been Lina's lifelong dream to become a published author.